Lawn Mower MAGiC

Lawn Mower
MAGiC

by Lynne Jonell
illustrated by Brandon Dorman

A STEPPING STONE BOOK™
Random House 🏠 New York

For Chris, who mowed his share of lawns—L.J.

For my grandfather, who was so patient with me
as his twelve-year-old lawn mower—B.D.

This is a work of fiction. Names, characters, places, and incidents either are the
product of the author's imagination or are used fictitiously. Any resemblance to
actual persons, living or dead, events, or locales is entirely coincidental.

Text copyright © 2012 by Lynne Jonell
Cover art and interior illustrations copyright © 2012 by Brandon Dorman

Published in the United States by Random House Children's Books,
a division of Random House, Inc., New York. Originally published in hardcover in
the United States by Random House Children's Books, New York, in 2012.

Random House and the colophon are registered trademarks and
A Stepping Stone Book and the colophon are trademarks of Random House, Inc.

Visit us on the Web!
SteppingStonesBooks.com
randomhouse.com/kids

Educators and librarians, for a variety of teaching tools,
visit us at RHTeachersLibrarians.com

The Library of Congress has cataloged the hardcover edition of this work as follows:
Jonell, Lynne.
Lawn mower magic / by Lynne Jonell ; illustrated by Brandon Dorman. — 1st ed.
p. cm. — (Magical mix-ups ; #2)
"A Stepping Stone book."
Summary: When Derek Willow is invited to visit a friend in the old neighborhood,
he and his siblings Abner, Tate, and Celia try to earn money for his train ticket
using an enchanted, and very hungry, lawn mower.
ISBN 978-0-375-86661-6 (trade) — ISBN 978-0-375-96661-3 (lib. bdg.) —
ISBN 978-0-375-86617-3 (pbk.) — ISBN 978-0-375-89673-6 (ebook)
[1. Lawn mowers—Fiction. 2. Magic—Fiction. 3. Brothers and sisters—Fiction.
4. Moving, Household—Fiction.] I. Dorman, Brandon, ill. II. Title.
PZ7.J675Law 2012 [E]—dc22 2010041058

Printed in the United States of America
10 9 8 7 6 5 4 3 2 1

Contents

CHAPTER I

Lawn Mower Trouble

No one would play football with Derek. No one would play kickball. No one would play soccer, even if he let them start two goals ahead. It was making him crazy.

"How about baseball, then?" Derek tipped back his head to call up into the climbing tree. High above, he spotted his brother's feet through the leaves. "Come *on*, Abner!"

"I'm busy." Abner eyed a branch above him. He was trying to see how high he could go.

As the oldest of the four Willow children, it was his duty to make sure the branches would hold everyone's weight. Besides, if a branch cracked just a little, it might be exciting.

Derek tipped his head so far back that his baseball cap fell off. He caught it neatly before it hit the ground. "But baseball is fun!"

"Not on this hill, it isn't," said Tate, his older sister. She looked up from her book and calmly turned a page. "The ball keeps rolling down to the river."

"It's more fun than climbing trees, or reading, or—" Derek glanced at his little sister, Celia. She seemed to be mashing a bottle cap on her stuffed rabbit's nose. "What *are* you doing, anyway?"

"Giving Mr. Bunny some milk, of course." Celia wrinkled her forehead at Derek. "I'm not playing baseball with you, either. You always make me stand in the outfield. And then I have to run after every single ball."

Derek squatted down and adopted a soothing tone. "Listen, Celia. It's just that you're so *good* at running after the ball, see?"

"It's not fair. And Mr. Bunny thinks so, too." Celia smoothed the blue satin ribbon that was tied around her stuffed animal's neck. She was glad Mother had finally unpacked the box that had held Mr. Bunny. The moving men had stuffed him in with the gardening tools by mistake.

Derek picked up the rabbit by the ears. "Face it, Mr. Bunny. What else is she going to do? She can't bat. And she sure can't catch."

"I can too catch," said Celia, leaping for her rabbit.

Derek tossed the rabbit over his head. It hit a branch and came down, legs flopping, into his ready hands. That gave Derek an idea. "Hey! Let's play bunny-ball!" he said.

"Give him back!" Celia cried.

Tate looked up from her book. "Stop being mean, Derek."

Abner called down from the tree, "Pick on somebody your own size. Go get the mail if you want something to do."

Derek, half-ashamed, tossed the stuffed rabbit to his little sister. He wasn't really trying to be mean. He just wanted to play something fast and exciting. Bunny-ball might have been fun. And there *wasn't* anybody his own size—that was the problem.

Derek scuffed down the long, winding driveway to the mailbox. Maybe his plastic army men had come in the mail. Two weeks ago he had sent off some cereal box tops. Every day since, he had waited for a package. It was a dusty trip to the mailbox and a hard climb back up the hill, but at least it was something to do.

He missed his friends. Back in his old neighborhood, if he wanted a game, all he ever had to do was step out the door. There was always something fun going on—street hockey, tetherball, basketball, even mudball, if it had just rained.

Mrs. Willow did not like mudball. She said she could never get Derek's clothes clean. But mudball was the best. You got extra points if the ball landed in a mud puddle, and you could play it with almost any sport.

Derek loved getting dirty, and he loved playing hard. But ever since they had moved to this lonely house on a hill, there was no one to play with. Except Abner, Tate, and Celia, of course. It just wasn't the same.

The branch above Abner's head creaked, and he hastily let it go. He watched through the leaves as his brother trudged over the stone arch bridge, threw a stick into the river, and ran to the big silver mailbox on the main road.

He supposed he really should play catch with Derek. But just throwing a ball back and forth was boring. He would rather be up in this tree. No one could see him, but he could see everything that was going on. It was like he was a secret spy.

He could see into the third-story windows of their house at the top of the hill. He could see his father walking from the house to the garage. He could see the garden shed and the toolshed. He could even see the small shed where his mother painted the pictures she hoped to sell one day. She called it her studio, but it still looked like a shed to Abner.

There was a banging noise as Father flung open the big wooden door to the garage. A moment later, he came out again, dragging the lawn mower.

Abner stopped being a spy at once. He slid down the tree trunk, jumped from the lowest branch, and landed on the ground with a thud. He eyed the battered red mower with longing. "I wish he'd let me mow, for once," he said out loud. "I'm responsible enough."

Mr. Willow yanked at a cord. There was a faint rattle, and then nothing. He bent over the elderly machine and fiddled with a lever, muttering something that Abner could not hear.

Tate glanced up from her book again. "It never starts on the first try," she said.

"Or the second," said Abner as their father pulled the cord again, harder.

The machine coughed twice and died.

"Poor Daddy." Celia patted her stuffed rabbit's ears. "Mr. Bunny feels sorry for him, too."

Derek came puffing up the hill. His pockets
were jammed with envelopes. "No package.
No army men," he said briefly.

"Any letters for us?" asked Tate. She closed
her book.

"I didn't even look. I mean, when are there
ever any letters for us?" Derek pulled the envelopes out of his pockets and handed them

over. "Here. It's probably just bills." He threw himself down on the long grass.

"It's always bills," said Celia. She had heard her father say this more than once.

The mower sputtered to life at last and Mr. Willow pushed it forward, sweating in the hot sun.

"Fifth try," said Abner. He had been ticking them off on his fingers. "One of these days it's not going to start at all."

"I wish new lawn mowers didn't cost so much," Tate said. She flipped through the envelopes one by one. Someday there *might* be a letter for one of them.

"I bet Dad wishes he was cutting the grass at our old house," Derek said. "There wasn't so much of it. This lawn is way too big."

It was true that there was a lot of lawn to mow. There was a narrow strip of short grass where their father had mown. But beyond that, a vast expanse of shaggy green covered the hill.

"Our old house didn't have a river, though," said Tate.

"Or good climbing trees," said Abner.

"Or *magic*," added Celia.

There was a moment of silence. It had been weeks since magic had happened on that very hill.

"Maybe it will never happen to us again," said Derek, who was feeling gloomy.

"Lots of kids never have magic happen to them even once," Abner pointed out.

Tate looked down at the envelopes in her hand and turned over the last few. "We should feel lucky," she said.

The Willow children tried to feel lucky. They were only partly successful.

"You can feel lucky for a while," said Celia, swinging Mr. Bunny by one foot, "but then you stop feeling lucky and you start wanting something else to happen."

This was so very true that no one bothered to comment.

But suddenly something else did happen.

"You got a letter!" Tate cried. "Look, Derek!" She handed a square envelope to her brother.

Derek tore it open and stared with unbelieving joy.

"What? What does it say?" Celia and Abner crowded in close.

Derek read the scrawled invitation once more and grinned until his cheeks hurt. His friend Ben wanted him to come for a birthday party and stay for a week! A whole week in the old neighborhood, with the guys! He would pack his baseball glove, and his bat, and his hockey stick!

Tate leaned over Derek's shoulder and read aloud. "'Let us know which train you're taking, and my parents will meet you at the station.'" She looked up. "You'll have to buy a round-trip ticket. How much money do you have in your piggy bank?"

Derek's grin faded. "Six dollars and thirty-seven cents . . . I think."

"Not enough," said Abner. "Round-trip tickets cost a lot of money."

Derek gripped the letter tightly. He watched his father, who was bent forward, pushing the mower hard uphill. Would his parents pay for the ticket? How much would it be?

The mower gave a sudden *POP* and belched a puff of oily smoke. Mr. Willow jumped back as it spit out a clump of grass. Then, with a rattle and a groan, it died. And nothing Father did made it go again.

The children stood at a respectful distance, as if at a funeral.

"Fine, then!" Mr. Willow wiped his forehead and glared at the machine. "Die, if you must. But where I'm going to find the money for a new lawn mower, I don't know."

CHAPTER 2

Grass Guzzler

"Sheep eat grass." Mr. Willow slumped on a stool inside the small shed that his wife had turned into an art studio. "We should get some sheep."

The children watched through the open doorway. Derek still clutched his invitation in his hand.

"But sheep cost money, too," said Mrs. Willow. She set her paintbrush down in a swirl of red. "And sheep wander off. Maybe the mower can be fixed again."

14

Mr. Willow put his head in his hands. "I remember thinking what a good place this was," he said. "Woods! A river! Lots of room for the kids to play! But did I look at the acres and acres of grass? Did I, even once, stop to think that it would just keep on *growing*?"

"Now, dear," said Mrs. Willow, patting her husband's arm.

"Even while we sleep, it grows!"

Tate backed away from the worried voices. She liked peace and calm above all things. She did not like it when people were upset.

A ring of slender trees circled the hill, like a tall, spiky crown. They were peaceful, those trees. They were not unhappy about money or broken mowers or round-trip tickets. Tate wanted her family to be as peaceful as the trees. She tried very hard to think of something she could do to make her family happy again.

"If only it had happened next month," her father's voice went on from a distance. "That wouldn't have been so bad. But this month, we're short of money. It cost a lot to move. And the university doesn't pay as well as my old job."

"Never mind the money." Mother's voice came faintly on the breeze. "This is a good chance for you to do important work, and it's just for a year. I could get a part-time job in town."

"But we agreed this would be your chance to paint!" Father's shoulders slumped. "I think we'll have to get out the credit cards after all."

Mother shook her head. "No, we promised each other we would only use them for emergencies. Why don't I drop off some paintings in town? The coffee shop said they would put them up and see if they sold."

The children drifted back to stand beside

Tate. Behind them, the voices of their parents went on in a low murmur.

Abner put both hands on his brother's shoulders and gave him a little shake. "You can't ask them for train ticket money *now*."

"I know it," said Derek miserably.

Celia stuck her thumb in her mouth. With the other hand, she held out Mr. Bunny to her brother.

This last kindness was too much for Derek. There was a hot feeling behind his eyes, and his face felt stiff. He yanked off his baseball cap, turned away, and pretended to fix the strap.

Tate thought she had better take charge before people started crying. "Blow your nose, Derek," she said. "And, Celia, take your thumb out of your mouth. You're not a baby anymore."

"I just forgot," said Celia with dignity. She dried her thumb on her shirt and looked at it fondly. It would still be there at bedtime if she needed it.

"I have an idea." Tate said this very firmly, to cover up the fact that she did not actually have a real idea yet. But she was hopeful that one would come to her soon.

"What?" everyone asked.

Tate stared at the lawn mower, still smoking slightly, and the wedge of cut grass behind it.

Her gaze traveled over the garage, past the trees, to the toolshed. And then, all at once, she *did* have an idea.

"Come on!" Tate took off across the hilltop.

"Where are you going?" Abner strode after her. Derek wiped his nose, jammed his cap back on, and ran to catch up. Celia followed more slowly. She was picking up handfuls of the cut grass for Mr. Bunny to eat.

Tate stopped on the cement slab in front of the toolshed door. She crossed her fingers for luck. Then she lifted the latch and pulled at the handle. Rusted hinges creaked as the big door swung open.

Inside, the shed was dark and dusty and full of junk—tools, yard equipment, tangled ropes. Derek and Abner crowded in after Tate and stood for a moment, letting their eyes adjust to the dim light.

"Cool!" said Derek. He picked up a long-handled blade that curved like a slice of lemon. "We could cut the grass with this!"

"Watch it!" Abner ducked. "Don't swing it around, Derek. You're going to take someone's head off."

"AHA!" Tate cried. She grasped a wooden handle in the corner and tugged. There was a clatter as two rakes and a pail fell to the floor. "I knew there had to be an old mower in here!"

The old-fashioned mower was like an overgrown and very dirty push toy. The long handle was connected to a reel of red blades and two dusty rubber wheels.

Abner squinted at it doubtfully. "That's a *really* old mower."

"Where's the gas tank?" asked Derek.

"It doesn't need gas," said Tate, standing up straight. Her cheeks were flushed, and her hair was coming out of its ponytail. "That's the best thing about it! There's nothing to break. All you do is hold the handle and push!"

"Really?" Derek gave the mower a little shove.

"I bet you'd have to push it *hard*," said Abner. He dragged the mower, clanking and thumping, out of the shed and onto the cement slab. "Watch out, Celia."

Celia had found a patch of clover for Mr. Bunny at the edge of the slab. She wasn't interested in the dirty mower.

It looked even worse in the sunlight. The wooden handle was worn and cracked. The long shaft was covered with cobwebs. And the blades were dull and rusty.

"Maybe it mows better than it looks," Tate said without much hope.

Abner kicked at one of the rubber wheels.

"Dad will never want to mow the whole hill with this old thing. It would take forever."

Derek bent down to brush the cobwebs away. "*I'd* mow with it," he said. "If Dad would let me, I'd mow the whole hill. Then he wouldn't have to buy a new mower this month. And he'd have enough money for my train ticket."

Abner and Tate exchanged a glance.

"You'd never be able to do it," said Abner.

"It would take you forever," added Tate.

Derek creased the party invitation between his hands. "I don't care how long it takes," he said, and he lifted his chin. But this was a mistake, because now he could see the shaggy lawn. And there was so *much* of it.

In his heart, Derek despaired. He would never get it all done. Before he got to the bottom of the hill, the top would have grown long again.

"Mr. Bunny will help," said Celia. She ripped up handfuls of grass and clover and threw them to one side, just like a mower. "Rabbits love to chew grass."

"Oh, right," said Derek bitterly. "Mr. Bunny's going to be a *big* help."

Scrrrreeeaaak . . . scrrrreeeaaak . . .

It was a dry, metallic sound, like two butter knives scraping together. Derek whipped around. There was nothing behind him but the shed and the rusty old mower. Only the mower was not quite as close to the shed as before.

Derek stared. Had the mower *moved*?

Tate frowned and set the machine back against the side of the shed. "Don't play with the lawn mower, Celia. You might hurt yourself."

"I didn't touch it!" said Celia.

Tate sighed. "Okay, then, don't let *Mr. Bunny* play with the mower."

Celia stuck out her lower lip. "Mr. Bunny didn't do anything. He's just eating grass, and I'm just throwing grass, like this—"

Scrrrreeeaaak . . . scrrrreeeaaak . . .

The children's attention snapped to the lawn mower. Four pairs of eyes grew wide as the curving blades scraped again. The wheels moved away from the shed a second time.

There was a sudden and alert silence.

"Do it again, Celia," said Abner, his voice strained.

Celia backed up. Then, feeling safer, she threw another handful of grass. Most of it missed the mower completely. But a little—a very little—fell on the rusty mower blades.

And the blades moved.

The children hardly dared to look at one another. Every heart leaped with a fearful joy. Was it true? Had magic, the deep magic that came from under the hill, happened to them again? Or—and this was the fearful part— were they somehow mistaken?

The mower had hardly moved, but the bits of grass wafted up from the blades as if caught in a tiny, curling breeze. They swirled about the children and fell back down to settle on the cement slab.

Celia took a breath and started to speak, but Tate clapped a hand over her mouth.

"Don't say it," Tate whispered fiercely. "Don't say the word until we're sure. We've got to test it."

Abner nodded. He bent down and ripped up two handfuls of grass. As if in a trance, Derek did the same.

"On three," said Abner. "One—two— three!"

The boys opened their fists above the

mower, and four clumps of fresh grass fell into the dull and rusty blades. The mower gave a rasping sound, like a metallic chuckle, and leaped forward.

CHAPTER 3

Mowey

"Look out!" cried Tate. She jerked Celia out of the way.

Abner stared in shock. The mower made a clever wiggle around him and rolled off the cement slab. With a whirring, chewing sound, it dug happily into the long grass.

"Catch it, Abs!" hissed Tate. "Before the parents see!"

The mower whipped from side to side as the wheels turned this way and that. Abner jumped forward, took three long strides, and grabbed the handle.

The machine settled down when it felt his touch. Abner swung around and the mower turned sweetly, heading back to the cement slab like a dog to its kennel. But it didn't stop when it bumped into the shed. It kept right on bumping, its wheels spinning, as if it couldn't believe there wasn't any more grass.

Derek had not moved. He gazed at the machine with awe.

"A lot of help *you* were," Abner said. He let the handle go and wiped his forehead.

Derek ignored this. "It wants to mow," he said happily. "It wants all the grass it can cut."

"It sure does." Abner scowled at the mower, which was still banging against the shed. "I wish it would calm down, though."

"I guess I can say the word *now*," said Celia. "It's *magic*!"

"It's better than that," said Derek, his eyes shining. "It's my train ticket home!"

"We've got to get Dad to agree first." Tate glanced across to the little studio where her parents were still talking.

"He'll never let us use it if it keeps bashing the shed!" Abner was exasperated.

"Why don't we just tell Daddy it's magic and let him mow?" Celia asked. "I bet it will go faster than the gas mower."

"I bet it will, too," said Tate. "But don't you see? Dad *can't* believe in magic—he's a grown-up. He'll just think there's something strange and wrong about it. For sure he'll think it's too dangerous to use something he doesn't understand."

"Magic *is* dangerous," said Abner. He eyed

the mower, which was ramming a good-sized dent in the side of the shed. "Maybe we shouldn't use it, either."

"Come *on*, Abner!" Derek begged for the second time that day. "It's not dangerous. It's just been cooped up too long. You're happy to be outside again, aren't you, Mowey?"

"Mowey?" mouthed Tate.

"Okay," said Abner. "Maybe if we put the mower in the shed, it will quiet down. If we can get it to stay still, Dad will think it's a regular mower and let us use it. Come on, Derek. Help me. Tate, will you hold the door? And, Celia, get out of the way."

"I always have to get out of the way," Celia mourned.

"That's because you're the littlest," said Derek. He grabbed one side of the mower handle.

"Careful," said Abner as the wheels spun. "Okay, let's back up into the shed. Pull."

"I'm not the littlest," Celia protested. "Mr. Bunny is."

"That's right," said Tate, opening the door wider as both boys squeezed through. "You have to stay out of the way so you can keep Mr. Bunny safe."

"Oh." Celia watched as the mower bumped up over the threshold and into the shed.

But the thumping noises didn't stop. And now there was clanking, too, and the sound of falling tools. Celia poked her head in. The mower was banging against the wall.

"Is it mad at us?" Celia asked. She wound Mr. Bunny's blue ribbon nervously around her fingers.

"It can't get mad," Abner said. "It's a lawn mower. Lawn mowers don't have feelings."

"Ordinary lawn mowers don't," Tate said. "*This* one might."

Derek caught a falling shovel and a fishing rod and propped them up again. "Maybe it's a little grumpy," he said. "It's like it's just waking up after a long sleep."

Celia looked at the restless mower. She thought she saw a bit of green. "Or maybe it still has some grass on the blades."

"Hey, I bet you're right!" Abner leaned over the mower, speaking above the steady *thud–thud–thud* as it bashed the wall. "But how can we get it off?"

"Don't put your hand in the blades, Abbie!" cried Tate.

"I won't," said Abner hotly. "I'm not stupid."

Celia tugged at Abner's shirt. "Mr. Bunny can help."

"Oh, give it a rest, Celia." Abner shrugged her off.

"No, really! He can!"

"Quiet, Celia!" Tate said. "We're trying to think!"

Abner stuck his head out of the shed and pulled it back in with a dismayed look on his face. "The parents are coming!"

"Mr. Bunny can *help*," Celia said stubbornly. She unwound the rabbit's neck ribbon and held it out. "This can dust off the blades."

"Right!" Derek grabbed the ribbon and doubled it over. Then he whapped it across the mower blades, lightly and fast.

"Careful!" Tate said, but Derek didn't bother to answer. The blades were already slowing down. And then, after a last quick dusting, they stopped.

"Just in time!" whispered Abner as grown-up feet scraped on the cement slab. "Good work, Derek."

"It was *my* idea," Celia reminded them as she took back the ribbon.

"What was your idea?" said Mother at the door.

"And what was all that noise?" asked Father. "It sounded like the whole shed was coming down!"

Abner turned to Tate. So did Derek and Celia. When something had to be explained to grown-ups, Tate was the one who did it best.

"The noise was because of the idea," she said earnestly. "We thought there might be a mower here you could use. And we found one and pulled it out, and then some of the other tools and things fell down. The mower made them fall," she added, being perfectly truthful.

Abner looked at her in admiration.

Mr. Willow glanced at the rusty lawn mower and shook his head. "That was good of you kids, but there's more lawn on this hill than I have time to mow with a push mower. Your mother and I are going into town. She's going to drop off some paintings, and I'm going to look at new lawn mowers. I'll see if the old one can be fixed, but I doubt it's possible."

"Dad?" Derek tugged at his father's sleeve. "Could I mow?"

"With the new mower? No, they're too dangerous," began his father.

"I meant with this one." Derek patted the old-fashioned mower's handle as if it were a friendly dog. "It's not dangerous at all. And I really want to."

"But whatever for?" asked Mother. "This hill is far too big for a boy your age to mow. That's your father's job."

"But if I did mow the whole hill, could I get money for it?" Derek persisted. "Enough to buy a train ticket?" He dug in his pocket and handed them Ben's invitation.

Mother finished reading first. She raised her head and looked sadly at her son. "Oh, Derek. You must want to go very much."

Derek nodded twenty times or so.

Father's face changed. Derek could not be sure if his father's expression was more stern or more loving, but it was more *something*. He waited, shifting from one foot to the other like a nervous batter at the plate.

Father cleared his throat. "I admire your ambition, son," he said. "But the fact remains that the hill is very large, and you are very small."

"He's not *that* small," Abner said.

"And we'll help him," said Tate.

The four children moved closer together.

Four pairs of eyes pleaded with Mr. and Mrs. Willow.

"All right," said Father. "You can try that old mower if you like, but you'll get tired of pushing it before long. I'm going into town to look at new lawn mowers."

"But what if we don't get tired?" Abner spoke up. "What if you come back from town and the mowing is all done? Would that earn enough money for Derek's ticket?"

"Er . . . ," said Father, looking helplessly at his wife.

"You always tell us not to give up before we start," added Derek.

"Please, Daddy?" Celia held up her rabbit. "Don't buy a new mower until you see if we can do it. Mr. Bunny says 'please,' too."

"Oh, good heavens," muttered their father.

"You're outnumbered, Frank," Mrs. Willow

said. She seemed to be trying not to laugh.

Tate sensed the tide was turning in their favor. "How about this," she said. "You go to town and look at mowers, but don't buy any. And then when you come home, you can see how much we've done."

"Not much point in going to town if we don't buy anything," grumbled their father.

"Now listen," said his wife, "we wouldn't buy a mower today, anyway. You know you always like to sleep on these things. You never make the final decision until the next day."

"That's true," Father admitted.

"And I think we should let the children try," Mother went on. "They want to do a nice thing for their brother, and . . . Well, if they did mow the whole lawn, you have to admit it would be worth a train ticket. Don't you agree?"

CHAPTER 4

Hang On!

Mother leaned out of the car window, giving final instructions. "Now be careful! Drink plenty of water, and stop if you get overheated. I don't want anyone getting sick."

"We promise," said the children all together.

"Stop worrying," said Father. "They'll be just fine."

"Why don't you come with us to town, Seal?" Mother reached out a hand to her youngest daughter, calling her by her baby name. "They won't need you to help mow."

Celia hesitated. Going to town with her parents usually meant stopping for ice cream cones. But she didn't want to be left out of the magic.

Abner and Tate glanced at one another. Celia *wouldn't* be much help. And the last time they had run into magic, she had caused some big problems.

"But we *do* need her," Derek blurted out. Then he stopped in confusion. Why had he said that?

Celia beamed.

"All right," said Mother, pulling her head back in the car. "Promise me that you won't let Celia mow. She's too little."

"We *promise*," everyone chorused again.

"You're worrying about nothing," Father told Mother as he put the car into gear.

"They'll quit before half an hour is up. Pushing a hand mower is a lot harder than they think."

❧❧❧

The children watched as the family car rolled down the long driveway, bumped over the stone arch bridge, and roared off down the gravel road. From the high hill, they could see all the way to the crossroads. That was where their mother usually remembered something she had forgotten.

They held their breath. But the car turned onto the main highway, its dark blue roof glinting in the sun.

Abner went into the shed and backed out, pulling the mower. "Okay, Celia, you stay out of the way." The wheels thumped down onto the cement slab, and he turned to Derek. "Listen. It's not hard. The mower does the work, but you have to hold on tight."

"And mow in a straight line," said Tate, "like Dad does. Don't let it wiggle all over the place."

Derek nodded. His chest felt tight and his breath came quickly. It was the way he always felt before throwing the first pitch in baseball, or kicking off in football, and it was a feeling he loved. "Okay, Mowey—let's go!" He gripped the handle, stiffened his elbows, and pushed the mower off the cement.

For a moment, he thought it wasn't going to work. Then all at once the handle shuddered, and the blades bit at the thick green grass. Derek yelped as the lawn mower surged ahead like a dog straining at the leash.

"Settle down now! Straighten it out," he yelled, wrestling the mower out of its zigzag path.

There was a lot of grass, but the mower was

more than up to it. After its long sleep in the toolshed, it almost pranced through the thick lawn. Its blades whirred with a quiet, satisfied sound, and grass spit out behind it like chopped salad. Derek felt proud, steering the headstrong machine across the yard. Behind him, he heard the others cheering.

He saw a tree ahead and leaned hard to one side to circle the trunk. The mower resisted at first. Once it got the idea, it seemed to like going round and round. Derek was dizzy before he figured out how to dig in his heels and swing the mower off at an angle.

It was almost as good as an amusement park ride. Better, thought Derek as he circled another tree, because at the end of it he would have earned enough money for a train ticket. He could hardly wait to see the guys.

The mower seemed to be speeding up.

Maybe it was only now fully awake, or maybe some of the rust had chipped off. Either way it was going faster than he wanted to go. Round and round, back and forth, it kept right on mowing and it wouldn't stop.

Derek's arms felt tired from gripping the handle so tightly. His legs didn't want to walk another step, much less run.

Where were the others? He could use a break. "Abner!" he tried to shout. "Tate!" But he was so out of breath that his voice was hardly more than a whisper.

Maybe they had gone to the house to get him some water. Derek hoped so with all his heart. It was hot out in the sun, and his baseball cap had fallen off.

In the kitchen, Abner, Tate, and Celia had decided to make lemonade. Their mother liked the real thing instead of the powdered kind, so she kept a bag of lemons on hand. The children were squeezing them and making a mess.

Celia spilled the sugar, and the mess got worse. Then she stirred too hard, and the lemonade splashed out and wet the sugar on the floor. When she tried to help clean up, she slipped and knocked over the wash bucket. Soapy water flooded everywhere.

Tate stood with her hands on her hips. Abner reached for a towel.

"I'm sorry," said Celia. "I was just trying to help."

Tate picked up a sponge. "You'll help us more if you stay out of the kitchen."

Celia sat in the front hall and watched

through the window as Derek went past with the mower.

Why had Derek said they needed her? They weren't going to let her mow. And now that she had spilled the sugar, they wouldn't even let her help make lemonade.

Celia held a sticky Mr. Bunny close as she watched Derek come around again. He was walking quickly. In fact, he was trotting. As he passed, he seemed to be yelling something.

Celia thought for a minute. Then she went back to the kitchen. "Derek's mowing *fast*," she told her brother and sister.

Abner was on his knees, wiping the floor with a dish towel. "He's got to mow fast if he wants to get it all done."

"No," said Celia, "I mean *really* fast. I think he needs help."

Tate pushed the hair out of her flushed face.

"He probably just needs someone else to take a turn. I'll go, Abner."

Tate stepped out the door, but Derek whipped by before she could do anything.

"I told you," said Celia as a long, drawn-out "Taaaaaaate!" drifted back from behind their brother.

"Wow," said Tate.

"Get ready," said Celia. She stood at the corner of the house. "Here he comes again."

Tate got into a half-crouch and held her arms out. The whirring sound of the mower got louder. As Derek went by, she grabbed the handle and took off with a jerk.

Derek let go with a groan of relief. He fell down flat on the cut grass.

Celia bent over him. "Do you want some lemonade? There's some in the house."

Derek nodded weakly. He felt as if he had

played too long without a substitute.

The door slammed behind Celia, and Derek sat up. He had mown an amazing amount in a short time. The top of the hill was shorn, and the long grass around trees and outbuildings was neatly trimmed. Down below, the lawn was still shaggy, but the mower did not seem to be getting tired. In fact, the more it mowed, the faster it seemed to go.

When would it quit? Derek wondered. Maybe they could try to stop it by running it into the shed again. But the mower would keep right on bashing until they dusted off the grass. The last time, Mowey had almost banged a hole in the wall before they got it to stop. If the shed had to be fixed, that would cost money, too. Would it cost as much as a train ticket?

Derek found the strength to stand up and totter into the house. He gulped down two

glasses of tart lemonade. When he stopped at
last, he told Abner and Celia what he had
been thinking.

At the sink, Abner wrung out a sponge. "I wonder why the magic settled in the mower? The mower wasn't underground, in a burrow."

The others nodded, remembering. The last time magic had happened to them, they had found out that it seeped up from deep in the earth. It came from somewhere under the hill on which their house stood. But they had thought the magic only affected small animals living in burrows.

Mowey had not been in the ground, soaking up magic. It had lived aboveground, for years, in a shed.

"Maybe the shed is like a burrow," said Celia. "It's dark and sort of closed-in."

"I suppose the magic could come up through the floor of the shed," said Abner, remembering the holes in the floorboards. "And maybe it got into the mower? I don't know.

Magic is hard to figure out." He shrugged.

Suddenly Abner's eye was caught by some sort of motion. He dropped the sponge and went to the window. All he saw was the flutter of Tate's long brown hair, and then it was gone.

They hurried outside. Tate, hanging on grimly, was running after the mower with great long strides, like a gazelle.

"I'd better take a turn," muttered Abner, worried. He was the biggest, and if he couldn't control it, what could they do? "Maybe we should put it in the shed for a while."

But the mower did not seem to like this idea. It gave a sudden twist and hopped to the side just as Abner reached for it. Mowey took off again, faster than ever.

"We'll block for you," said Derek. "Celia, get on the other side. Get ready. . . . Get set. . . . Hut one! Hut two!"

The mower tried to scoot around Abner, but Derek chased it back. It tried to jump to the other side, but Celia was there, waving Mr. Bunny. And then it was too late for the mower to escape, because Abner grasped the handle.

It nearly slipped from his fingers, but he hung on somehow, leaping over Tate as she collapsed. At once he was off and mowing, his long legs taking the lawn mower's speed in stride.

The others carried the pitcher of lemonade down to the shed and sat on the cement slab. They watched as Abner went round and round. Each time his legs seemed to be moving faster than before.

"It's a good thing we never let you try it, Celia," Tate said. She took a swallow from her glass.

"*I* barely made it." Derek wiggled his toes in the grass. "My legs were starting to cramp."

"He's coming back to the shed," said Celia suddenly. She jumped up to open the door.

But the mower was in no mood to go in the shed. It curved away just as soon as it was in sight of the cement slab, and gave a rusty little chortle.

"Grab on!" cried Abner. "Help me slow it down!"

Tate waited for her chance. And when Abner came around again, she ran with him,

matching his steps—or nearly—until she could
reach out and take hold of his belt. She hung
on with two hands and tried to use her weight
to slow Abner down. The mower just threw
itself more seriously into its work.

"We need one more!" cried Tate as they
came around again.

Derek leaped up, knocking over his glass
of lemonade. He took a running jump and
hooked his fingers into the top of Tate's jeans.

Celia watched. The mower was not slowing down. They would need her, too.

She took Mr. Bunny's blue satin ribbon and knotted one end tightly around his arm. Then she tied the other end around her belt loop. When her sister and brothers called, she would have both hands free.

"Ceeeeeeliaaaaa!" came the cry.

Celia crouched. She was ready.

"Get *out* of the *waaaaaay!*"

The mower was going so fast, the children's feet were a blur. It hit a bump, leaped into the air, and shook off the children like a tree tossing off apples in a high wind.

Abner, Tate, and Derek tumbled to the grass, *thump thump thump*. And the mower, with a scraping snort, bounced once on its rubber tires and disappeared over the hilltop.

CHAPTER 5

A Mind of Its Own

But when the children ran to the top of the hill and looked over its steep side, the mower was behaving perfectly. It had found a patch of long grass and was busily clipping it short.

Abner glared down at the mower. "Sure, it looks all innocent *now*. Just wait until we try to stop it again."

"Why do we need to stop it?" Celia asked.

Abner rubbed his sore shoulder. "Think, Seal. What if it's still mowing when Mom and

Dad get home? How are we going to explain that?"

Celia saw the problem. It was hard enough to explain ordinary things, like spilling the sugar and getting the kitchen floor all sticky. They would never be able to explain a magic mower, not in a million years.

"It will be simpler if we don't have to explain at all." Tate touched the back of her head where a lump was rising, and winced. "But we need a better way to stop that lawn mower. My head hurts."

Derek blew on his scraped knee. "I'm bleeding."

"We all are," Abner said. "Mowey plays rough."

"Come on, I'll get some bandages." Tate turned toward the house. "Celia, you watch the mower. Tell us if it does anything it shouldn't."

"Like what?" Celia asked.

"Anything besides mowing the lawn," Tate said.

"*Our* lawn," Abner added hastily. "Not anybody else's."

Celia climbed onto a large, flat rock on the crest of the hill. She lay on her stomach and peered over the edge. Down below was the steeper, wilder side of the hill. The Willow children did not play there, because it was full of stickers. The bushes had thorns, too, and there was a pile of old, rusted metal that Mrs. Willow said was dangerous.

But the mower went happily back and forth, cutting anything green it could find. It hopped over small rocks and circled around big ones. It did not try to mow the sand by the river, and it did not bump into the junk pile. It was acting exactly the way a lawn mower should.

Celia did not see why she had to watch it.

"Anyway," she told Mr. Bunny, "the magic will get used up after a while, I bet. Like that time with Hammy. Don't you remember?"

Celia made Mr. Bunny shake his head from side to side.

"Oh, that's right," Celia said. "You were still packed in a moving box the last time the magic happened." She told Mr. Bunny the story of how Hammy, their pet hamster, had used up all his magic with one very big wish. It was a long story. Celia made Mr. Bunny put his paws over his mouth at the exciting parts.

The wind moved in the trees that circled the hilltop, and Celia shifted on the rock. This was getting boring. And it was hot.

She wished the mower would hurry up and finish. Why was it playing around on the wild side of the hill? No one cared if it mowed the weeds.

Celia stood up on the rock and turned around. The grass was short at the top of the hill, around the buildings, and along the winding driveway. But down beyond the vegetable garden, near the tall hedge, there was more grass that Mowey had not touched.

"Hey!" Celia waved at the mower. "There's more to mow on the other side!"

Mowey was attacking a thick patch of weeds. But when Celia called, it stopped. Its handle twitched.

"Follow me!" cried Celia. She jumped off the rock. Mr. Bunny, still tied to her belt loop, jumped with her.

Celia marched across the hilltop. She could hear the whirring, scraping sound of the lawn mower behind her. She passed the house and her mother's art studio and waited in the shade of the open garage. "There!" Celia pointed. "Go mow that, why don't you?"

The mower moved slowly over the short grass. Celia threw some extra grass clippings into the blades as it passed, and it sped up a little.

She felt proud. The mower obeyed her! It wouldn't do what Derek said, or Tate, or even Abner. But it listened to her!

She did a little victory dance with Mr. Bunny in the garage. She danced around the red wagon and over Derek's hockey stick. She picked up a badminton racket and waved it over her head. And then she heard Abner shout.

"Mowey! Stop!"

Celia peeked out of the garage, still holding the racket. Abner, Tate, and Derek were running from the house.

"Chase it off!" cried Tate. "It's in the vegetable garden!"

Celia sucked in her breath. The garden was one of the ways their family was trying to save money this year. They could not grow their own vegetables if the garden was mown to bits.

"I'll block it!" Derek rushed the mower, waving his arms. The lawn mower reared back with a startled clank, ran over a cabbage, and spun into a patch of beets.

Abner leaped over a row of string beans and dove for the handle. But the mower had a new trick. It bobbed its handle just out of reach. Then it whirled around and bumped Abner's legs behind the knees. Abner fell over.

"NO! BAD MOWER!" Tate grabbed the racket from Celia's hand and ran to the garden. She swung the racket like a bat, and the mower flinched. "Back off!" she shouted. "Go over

there!" She pointed to the long grass by the hedge.

Celia watched as the mower went grumbling off. She had told the mower to find the long grass, too, but it had found the vegetable garden first. She did not feel quite so proud of herself anymore.

The mower, looking sulky, was mowing the patch of grass. But every so often it turned a little. Celia thought it might be looking at the lettuces.

What would it do after it finished with the grass?

Celia put her thumb in her mouth. That was how she did her best thinking. After a minute she went into the garage again. She picked up the badminton net.

When she came out, her sister and brothers were there. They did not seem happy.

"You were supposed to be watching Mowey," said Abner.

"Why didn't you call us?" Tate put her hands on her hips.

Derek pointed to the net in Celia's hands. "And *now* you want to play sports? When the mower is going nuts?"

"It's not for sports." Celia dried her thumb off on her shirt. "It's for catching Mowey. See?" She spread it out on the grass.

Tate nodded slowly. "Good thinking, Seal." She picked up one end of the net.

"Cool!" Derek said. "It will be like catching a wild animal or something!" He grabbed hold of the net in the middle.

"I hope it works," said Abner. He hooked his fingers through the other end. "Let's go!"

Celia skipped to catch up with them. "I want to help, too."

"No you don't," said Abner over his shoulder. "We promised Mom and Dad that you wouldn't mow."

"It was my idea to use the net," Celia said stoutly. She wove her hand through the mesh as they trotted single file, carrying the net between them like a long banner. "Besides, I'm not going to mow. I'm going to help you *stop* mowing."

"That's true," Tate said from behind.

"And we need all the help we can get," Derek added. "Look!"

They looked. And then they ran. The lawn mower had finished the patch of grass and was heading right back to the vegetable garden. The carrot tops looked like long, frilly grass. They waved in the light breeze.

Mr. Bunny was still tied to Celia's belt loop. He flopped at her side as she ran. Celia wanted to tell him to hang on, but she was out of breath.

"Get ready," Abner said. "Spread out!"

The mower's handle jerked up. Mowey seemed to hesitate, turning this way and that, as if wondering which way to go. It backed up until it was almost to the hedge. The children held the net up between them and moved closer . . . closer.

"Now!" cried Abner.

They flung the net over the mower. The handle whipped back but it caught in the webbing. Mowey tried to surge ahead, but the net snagged in the blades and over one wheel. The lawn mower spun in circles, dragging all four children behind it.

"Ow! Ow! Ow! Ow!" cried Celia as she bumped over the lawn. She was getting dizzy.

All at once the blades bit through the thin

strands of the net, and the wheel was free. The mower shook itself and roared straight ahead.

CRASH! It hit the hedge, hard.

Tate thought fast. "Turn it on its side so it can't mow!" she ordered.

"Good idea," grunted Abner. He flipped the mower on its side and pushed until it was trapped against the tall box hedge. "Now it can't go anywhere!"

The children sat in the shade of the box hedge, breathing hard. The mower was still, as if it had been stunned. One rubber tire was against the ground. The other tire was up in the air, spinning slowly.

Abner wound the net more tightly around the lawn mower's handle. "Now everybody grab the net and keep holding on," he said. "Just in case."

Tate patted the handle lightly. "It's not

a bad mower," she said. "It just gets a little
excited now and then."

"Only when it has something to mow,"

Abner said. "It gets slower when it's on grass that's already cut. And it stops when there's no grass at all."

"It just wants to do its job." Derek couldn't keep a grin off his face. Mowey had mown the whole yard, almost. He was going to get that train ticket for sure. He could hardly wait to play sports with the guys.

Celia smoothed Mr. Bunny's fur. He had gotten a little rumpled in all the excitement. She started to untie him, but Abner began to speak.

"The parents are going to come home soon," he said. "So here's what I think we should do. Celia, you get the red wagon from the garage. We will hold the mower here. We can use the wagon to take it to the shed. Then it won't touch any grass on the way back."

"Okay," Celia said. She could untie Mr.

Bunny later. Right now, her brothers and sister needed her.

"Hang on to the net," Abner warned Tate and Derek as Celia started toward the garage. "We have to keep the lawn mower trapped."

Derek tangled his hands more deeply into the mesh. "Look," he said. "I couldn't let go if I tried!"

A little breeze sprang up. The tiny leaves of the box hedge fluttered this way and that. They tickled at the edge of the mower blades, but the children did not notice.

"There's a last strip of grass across the driveway," said Derek. "It goes down to the river. Maybe we could let Mowey do that last bit?"

"NO!" said Tate.

Abner pushed the mower more firmly against the hedge. "I'm not letting Mowey get away from us again."

The breeze gusted, and the hedge leaves rustled against the blades once more. The mower made a small scraping sound, and then another. But the children did not hear. They were talking loudly.

"I was just kidding," said Derek.

"It wasn't funny," Abner said.

Tate shaded her eyes. "Here comes Celia with the wagon!"

But it was too late to use the wagon. The lawn mower had found something new to mow. With a quick rasp of metal, its blades started to whirl. Faster and faster they turned, chewing up the side of the leafy box hedge.

The children screamed.

"Don't let go!" Abner shouted.

"But it's going to mow right through the hedge!" cried Derek.

The handle bucked wildly. Tate tried to

stay calm. "It can't go *through* the hedge. Once it's past the leaves, there are only branches. It can't mow branches!"

"Hang on!" called Abner. "It's trying to shake us off!"

The mower whipped its handle from side to side. It shook it up and down. But Abner, Tate, and Derek did not let go of the tangled net.

Celia stopped pulling the wagon. Should she try to help? But no, she could see that they didn't need her. There was nowhere for the mower to go. Abner was on one side, and Tate was on the other. Derek was behind, and the hedge was in front. The only place the mower could go was—

Up.

Celia's mouth fell open. She gripped Mr. Bunny and watched as the mower roared straight up the hedge. Its handle was still

caught in the net, but it didn't seem to care. It had something green to mow, and it was going to mow it, no matter what.

Of course the three children were dragged behind.

"Hang on!" Abner shouted as he went up the side.

"Let go!" screamed Tate.

"I can't!" Derek cried. "I'm all tangled up!"

The mower reached the top of the tall hedge and plunged down the other side. One by one, the children went over the top, too. Celia saw their legs kicking, and then there was nothing left to see but a hedge with a wide bare strip from bottom to top.

CHAPTER 6

One for the Team

For a moment, Celia could not move. She almost forgot to breathe. Then she dropped the wagon's handle and ran toward the end of the long hedge. Her short legs pounded on the turf, and her heart was pounding, too.

If only her parents would come home! But there was no dark blue car coming up the driveway. There was no dust rising on the long dirt road that led from the highway to their mailbox. There was only a tractor in a field, moving slowly.

Celia got to the end of the hedge and peeked around the leafy corner. She did not want to get run down by a mower on the loose.

But the mower was not heading in her direction. It had mown straight down the other side of the hedge, dragging the children behind it. Now it was aiming for the last strip of long grass left on the hill. It hopped across the gravel driveway with hardly a stutter, and picked up speed on the other side, bouncing and clanking down the slope. The tag end of the badminton net flapped like a flag in a stiff breeze.

"STOP!" Abner's voice was getting hoarse, but he kept yelling anyway. Derek had stumbled, and Tate was trying to pull him to his feet again. Celia couldn't tell if they were caught in the net or just refusing to let go. But either way, her sister and brothers were being dragged like pull toys.

Celia was not big enough to stop the mower. But once before, she had called to the mower and it had followed her to a new patch of grass. Would it do the same thing again? Maybe she could fool it. If she could get it onto the stone bridge, there would be no grass for it to mow. It would slow down and maybe even stop. It was worth a try.

Celia patted Mr. Bunny's ears for luck. Then she ran up beside the mower. She smiled and waved. She made her voice sound high and happy. "Come on, Mowey! There's lots of grass over this way!"

"No—there—isn't—" Derek said, his words jerking out with every step. "Are—you—nuts?"

"Stay—away!" said Abner, galloping past. "Keep—safe—Celia!"

"But maybe—she's got—a plan!" Tate's voice trailed off as they ran.

Celia trotted down to the river's edge. Reeds were growing there, long and green. She yanked them up and waved them over her head. Then she pointed to the stone bridge and kept on waving. "MOWEY! OVER HERE! *LOTS* OF GRASS!"

The lawn mower hesitated. It turned toward Celia. Then it gave an eager hop. It tore down the last narrow strip of grass to the river, with Abner, Tate, and Derek bumping and yelling behind.

Celia jumped onto the bridge and ran halfway across. It was going to work! The mower had believed her! "COME ON, MOWEY!" she called. "COME TO THE *BRIDGE!*"

But the lawn mower did not go to the bridge. It went straight to the river, where the patch of reeds was the thickest. *Splash!*

It leaped into the water and churned ahead,
chewing up the reeds. *Splash! Splash! Splash!*
The three children were dragged into the river,
one after the other.

Celia did not know what to do. Were her brothers and sister going to drown? Her good idea had just made everything worse.

She looked around in a panic. Where were the grown-ups when she needed them?

And then she did see a grown-up. It was the farmer, on his tractor. He was not far away. Maybe she could get him to help.

Celia's sandals went *thwap thwap thwap* across the stone bridge. Mr. Bunny went *fuff fuff fuff* as he bounced against her side. She ran onto the gravel road and leaped across the ditch. She stumbled through the rows of alfalfa, waving her arms.

But the tractor was bigger than it had looked from a distance. It was very tall, and very loud. It was scary. She could not get close to it. And the farmer was looking the other way.

The tractor roared past. Celia clutched Mr.

Bunny to her chest, so hard that his ribbon broke. She turned around, almost afraid to look.

But her brothers and sister were not drowning. The mower was skimming over the water like a motorboat. Water sprayed back from the whirling blades and into the faces of the children floating behind. The droplets shone in the sun to make a rainbow.

Celia ran to the river's edge. How could Mowey keep on going when there was only water to mow?

When she got closer, she could see long reeds in the mower blades. Then she understood. The long reeds did not get chewed up as fast as grass. They kept the mower going, even in the water.

But the reeds were almost gone. The lawn was all cut short. Even Mowey seemed to understand this. Why else was it coming to her side of the river? There was only sand here, and a gravel road.

The children in the water looked wet and tired and worried. Celia wanted to cheer them up.

"It has to quit soon!" she called across the water. "There's nothing left for it to mow!"

Abner lifted his damp head and shook it. He said something over the whirr of the mower.

"What did you say?" Celia cupped her hand around her ear.

This time, Tate and Derek shouted along with Abner, "LOOK BEHIND YOU!"

Celia turned around. And then she saw what she had not noticed before.

The farmer's field of alfalfa was green and thick. It stretched as far as she could see. It looked like the biggest lawn in the world.

That was why the lawn mower was crossing the river!

Celia had to keep it from mowing the farmer's alfalfa. But how? Her brothers and sister had not been able to stop Mowey. Her parents were away from home. And the farmer had not even seen her.

All she had was Mr. Bunny. And Mr. Bunny couldn't do anything.

Or . . . could he?

Celia gasped. She had an idea! She was almost sure it would work. But she could hardly stand to think about it.

Mowey was chewing up the last few reeds on her side of the river. Soon it would roar up onto land again, and then—

Celia gulped. She bent her head and kissed Mr. Bunny under his chin, where he was softest. Then she whispered her idea in one of his long, silky ears.

Mr. Bunny did not shake his head to say

no. He looked at her with steady eyes.

"All right, then," Celia said. "You are a brave, brave rabbit."

She crouched. She watched. And when the lawn mower crunched up on the sand, Celia and Mr. Bunny did what they had to do.

Celia looked away. She couldn't watch. But she heard the mower choke. It gave a last rasping sigh, and then it stopped. No mower, not even a magic one, can keep on going when its blades are clogged with a stuffed rabbit.

Abner, Tate, and Derek slogged out of the river, dripping. They untangled themselves from the net. They stood in a circle around the mower, looking down.

"Wow," said Abner.

Derek patted Celia on the back. "Good old Mr. Bunny," he said. "He took one for the team."

Tate gave Celia a hug. "We'll give him a good funeral."

"A funeral?" Derek was indignant. "Listen, when a guy on a team gets injured, they don't bury him. They bring out the stretcher and take him to the hospital. Come on, Celia. Let's go get the wagon."

By the time Derek and Celia rattled the wagon over the bridge, the others had dusted every bit of green from the mower's blades. Abner lifted the mower into the red wagon. Slowly, carefully, he pulled at Mr. Bunny's paw. Bit by bit, the blades turned and the rabbit came free.

Abner handed what was left of Mr. Bunny to Celia. She tried very hard not to cry.

"Listen!" Derek said. "Do you hear the car?"

The dark blue sedan rolled up onto the bridge and stopped. Mr. Willow got out and stared at the freshly mown hill.

Mother got out, too, and gasped. "What on earth have you children been doing? You're all filthy, head to toe! And dripping wet! Have you been playing mudball?"

Derek grinned. Mowing the lawn with his brother and sisters had been *better* than mudball. It had been more exciting than any sport he had played in his life.

His father found his voice at last. "I don't believe it! I don't believe you mowed the whole thing!"

The children gazed up at the beautifully shorn hill.

"We can hardly believe it, either," said Tate.

There was a rumble from the nearby field as the tractor pulled up. A man with white hair climbed down and tugged at his cap. "Hi, folks. I saw your car, and thought I'd come meet the new neighbors. My name is Bud Wopter."

The grown-ups shook hands. They said the sort of things grown-ups always say when they meet. They talked about the weather. They

talked about their work. Mr. Wopter said he
sometimes did odd jobs around town, or for
neighbors.

Then the man said something interesting. He said that there had once been a mine under their house. "Yep. Hollowstone Mine, they called it."

Abner, Tate, Derek, and Celia were suddenly alert. The last time magic had happened to them, a hamster had said that their house was built on Hollowstone Hill. Was there really an old mine underneath their house?

Mr. Wopter scratched under his cap. "You might want to get your buildings tested," he said. "Living on top of a mine, and all. There might be radon, or something."

"Thanks," said Mr. Willow, "but I called ahead and had the buildings tested before we moved in. It's all safe."

"Might be other things besides radon," Mr. Wopter suggested. "I could check that for you. I have a special tester I rigged up. You never know what could be seeping up through the earth from that mine. I've heard some stories over the years—"

Mrs. Willow interrupted and put a hand on her husband's arm. "I'm sorry, but we need to get the children out of these muddy clothes."

"You just call me," said Bud Wopter, shaking Mr. Willow's hand. "Anytime." He nodded to Mrs. Willow, grinned at the children, and shambled off to his tractor.

"Honestly, that man!" said Mrs. Willow.

Mr. Willow chuckled. "He just wants an excuse to test his invention. I might even tell him to bring it over someday. He won't find any radon—"

"I should hope not!" said Mrs. Willow.

"—but he might discover a whole new element. Like, say, 'quack-ium'? Or maybe 'goof-ium'?"

"Weird-ium!" said Tate, getting into the spirit of things.

"Doof-ium!" suggested Abner.

"Or maybe *magic-ium*!" Celia whispered.

Mr. and Mrs. Willow laughed.

Derek decided he had better change the subject. "Dad? Did you look at new mowers?" he asked.

"Yes," said his father. "But we won't have to get one until the next paycheck, thanks to you kids." He gazed up at the hill again and shook his head in wonder. "You mowed the whole thing. I wouldn't have thought it was even possible. You must have been going at top speed the whole time!"

"We *were* going pretty fast," said Celia, remembering how dizzy she had gotten when the mower went in circles.

Mother's eyebrows went up. "But *you*

weren't supposed to be mowing, young lady."

"I wasn't," said Celia, and she felt this was true. She had been trying to *stop* the mower, which was a completely different thing. But she wasn't sure that her mother would understand this fine point.

Abner spoke up. "She never even touched the mower," he said. "Honest."

Mother frowned slightly. "But she said, '*We* were going fast.'"

"People always say 'we' when they're part of a team," said Derek. He clapped Celia on the shoulder. "Even if they're not on the field."

"And she helped us a lot," said Tate. "She made lemonade, for one thing." She smiled at her sister.

Celia was glad Tate hadn't mentioned the spilled sugar. She thought her mother would probably figure it out when her feet stuck to the kitchen floor, though.

"And what on earth happened to Mr. Bunny?" Mrs. Willow wanted to know.

Celia gazed down at the lumpy bundle in her hands. She was sad, but she was proud, too. Mr. Bunny had saved them from disaster.

She looked up at her mother. "He took one for the team."

CHAPTER 7

So Long, Farewell

They all went to the train station to see Derek off. Celia even brought Mr. Bunny, who was looking much better since Mother had mended him.

"You did a good job, Derek," said Father as he paid for the ticket. "I still can hardly believe you mowed the whole hill with that rusty old thing."

"I had a lot of help," said Derek. He shouldered his duffel bag and grinned at his brother and sisters.

Mr. Willow looked at his four children. "Well, I'm proud of you all. I didn't think it could be done, and yet somehow, some way, you did it. It was almost like—"

"Magic?" suggested Celia, stroking Mr. Bunny's somewhat crooked ears.

Mr. Willow laughed. "Well, magic *would* explain what happened to the hedge."

The children looked at one another guiltily.

"Now, Frank, don't start in on the hedge again!" said Mrs. Willow. "Come on, kids, up the steps now."

"But you've got to admit," her husband argued, "that the stripe in the hedge is the exact width of the mower. And it *did* appear the day the kids mowed the hill."

Mrs. Willow rolled her eyes as she climbed the stairs to the station platform. "So are you saying that the mower just drove itself straight up the hedge and then down again?"

Father looked embarrassed. "No, of course not."

"Or that any of the children did it? Because if that's what you think, then I'd like to see you explain *how*—"

"I'm not saying anything of the kind!" Father stamped up the train station stairs. "All I'm saying is, it's a mystery. I'd like to know what happened."

"Sometimes leaves fall off on their own," Tate said. "It's just one of those things."

"Maybe it was some kind of plant disease?" Mother sat on a platform bench. "Perhaps a sudden hedge fungus. Good heavens, Frank! Give it up. The leaves will grow back in time, I'm sure. And the children couldn't possibly have gotten that mower up and down the hedge, even if they'd tried."

"I know it. That's what's so strange," Mr. Willow muttered as the train pulled into the station with a metallic screech and a hiss of brakes.

"Here's your train, Derek," said his mother. "Hugs all around, and then off you go for a wonderful week in the old neighborhood!"

Hugs involving the Willow children were an energetic affair. But as Derek was getting his nose mashed and his shoulders squeezed and his foot stepped on, he suddenly felt glad that he would only be gone a week.

The whistle blew, and the conductor shouted, "All aboard!" Derek put his arms around his brother's and sisters' necks and pulled their heads close so that no one else could hear his whispered question. "What are you going to do if you find something else that's magic? While I'm gone, I mean?"

There was a pause. Everyone knew what Derek was really asking.

Abner shrugged. "We'll wait for you."

"We need a rest from magic, anyway," Tate said.

Celia gave her stuffed rabbit a squeeze. "Magic is tricky," she said. "Mr. Bunny says we need the whole team."

Derek grinned. "The rabbit's got a point," he said, and leaped onto the train.

The End

Look for more **Magical Mix-Ups** in

Grasshopper
MAGiC